1

I0571878

2

THE BEEBLES CONTINUANCE,
A Chord of Transition

by Lowery Christopher Collins

An optional, short play of transition
between "The Beebles Accord"
and "The Beebles Refrain"

4

THE BEEBLES CONTINUANCE,

A CHORD OF TRANSITION

BY LOWERY CHRISTOPHER COLLINS

Ponderlake Publishing

6

NOTICE

COPYRIGHT

CAUTION: Professionals and amateurs are hereby warned that performance of THE BEEBLES CONTINUANCE, A CHORD OF TRANSITION is subject to payment of a royalty and that all rights to this work are controlled exclusively by LOWERY CHRISTOPHER COLLINS, without whose permission in writing, no performance of it may be given. It is fully protected under the copyright laws of the United States of America and of all countries covered by the International Copyright Union and all countries with which the United States has reciprocal copyright relations. All rights, including amateur/stage rights, motion picture, recitation, lecturing, public reading, radio broadcasting, television, video and/or sound recording, Internet, and all other forms of mechanical or electronic reproduction, such as CD-ROM, CD-I, DVD, electronic or cloud storage, information storage and retrieval systems and photocopying, and the rights of translation into foreign languages, are strictly reserved.

Conscientious observance of copyright law is not only ethical, but it also encourages authors to continue creative work. No alterations, deletions, or substitutions may be may made in the work without the prior written consent of the author or his legal representative.

ROYALTIES and INQUIRIES

Royalty must be paid every time this play is performed whether or not it is presented for profit and whether or not admission is charged. A play is "performed" anytime it is acted before an audience.

All inquiries concerning any performance rights should be addressed to the playwright: L. Christopher Collins, P.O. Box 223, Carthage, Texas 75633 or mrchriscollins@hotmail.com.   Website: www.christophercollinsonline.com

CREDIT and ADVERTISEMENT

Anyone receiving permission to produce THE BEEBLES CONTINUANCE, A CHORD OF TRANSITION is required to give credit to the author as sole and exclusive author of the play on the title page of all programs distributed in connection with performances of the play and in all instances in which the title of the play appears for purposes of advertising, publicizing, or otherwise exploiting the play and/or a production thereof. The name of the author must appear on a separate line in which on other name appears, immediately beneath the title and in size and type equal to 50% of the size of the largest, most prominent letter used for the title of the play. No person, firm, or entity may receive credit larger or more prominent than that accorded the author.

THE BEEBLES CONTINUANCE,
A CHORD OF TRANSITION

Written by Lowery Christopher Collins

Copyright © 2020 by Lowery Christopher Collins

All rights reserved. No part of this book may be used or reproduced in any manner whatsoever without written permission except in the case of brief quotations embodied in critical articles and reviews. Printed in the United States of America. For information, contact Ponderlake Publishing, P.O. Box 223, Carthage, Texas 75633.

Ponderlake Publishing: www.ponderlake.com

Playwright and/or Royalty Information: www.ChristopherCollinsOnline.com

ISBN 978-0-9992241-3-7

This play serves as a transition piece between *The Beebles Accord* and *The Beebles Refrain*. While both plays may most certainly be performed without the production of this specific script, *The Beebles Continuance*, sandwiched between them, this particular play explains what occurs between the two larger plays and gives additional "continuance" to the plot line.

Either *The Accord* or *The Refrain* can be performed as its own independent production or they both can be performed in sequence with one another for a richer experience. Adding the supplemental *Continuance* between the productions provides even more to the story.

10

The Beebles Continuance,
A Chord of Transition
by Lowery Christopher Collins

5M, 2W

CAST OF CHARACTERS (in order of appearance)

Mary Ann

Brannon

Law

The Captain

Three Beach Characters (2 M, 1F)

12

PLEASE READ THESE NOTES BEFORE EVEN READING THE PLAY—

<u>Note About This SEQUEL:</u> This play, "The Beebles Continuance, A Chord of Transition," is an additional SEQUEL to "The Beebles Accord, a Dramatic Treatise of Time and Art" and a PREQUEL to "The Beebles Refrain, Another Testament of Time and Art." Although readers, producers, directors, actors, and even potential audiences are encouraged to have read or seen "The ACCORD" before watching or attempting "The CONTINUANCE" or "The REFRAIN," such a pre-knowledge is not necessary.

<u>Note About the PRODUCTION of the SHOW:</u> Note to potential directors: as is the case of "The Beebles Accord" or "The Beebles Refrain," when producing "The Beebles Continuance," please remember that while the shows being parodied should be done so with as much *fun and exaggeration* as possible, they must also be shown the proper <u>respect</u>. The show references are not mentioned to mock the plays, but rather to pay <u>homage</u> to them and to address them in a lighthearted manner. Also, while this play is, at times, farcical, please don't forget that it does contain <u>a message beyond the humor,</u> that all of us in the theatre world have a responsibility and an honor to create art on stage.

© 2020 Lowery Christopher Collins—All rights reserved.
mrchriscollins@hotmail.com / www.ChristopherCollinsOnline.com

14

THE BEEBLES CONTINUANCE,
A CHORD OF TRANSITION

The stage is black. There is silence. Slowly we can hear the sound of ocean waves getting louder and louder. Although the roar does not get very loud, the sound of ocean water lapping upon the shore can be distinctly heard. As the sound increases, we see an amber light slowly appear across the empty stage.

MARY ANN. (*Entering SR*) Hello? Hello? Is anybody around? Hey.

MARY ANN walks about the stage, looking left and right and even into the audience.

MARY ANN. Alone.

(As she sings, the stage lights come up.)

(Singing)

> I find the boards no longer beaten.
>
> I hear no chords the soul to sweeten.
>
> For the shades of what was here has fled away.
>
> And the set with all the glimmer,
>
> All the voices now grown dimmer:
>
> All are gone, and I feel led astray.
>
> Mary Ann, Mary Ann, you have gone astray.

A clapping comes from stage right and startles MARY ANN.

BRANNON. (*Entering*) Bravo!

MARY ANN. Brannon. I didn't think anyone was here.

BRANNON. You should have had your own solo in "The Accord."

MARY ANN. Fat chance of that happening.

BRANNON. Don't say that.

MARY ANN. Brannon, thank you, really, but I'm not the soloist. I could never be Piddles.

BRANNON. Of course not. And Piddles could never be you.

MARY ANN. You know what I mean. (*Beat*.) And I'm glad you're here. I thought something terrible had happened.

BRANNON. You are you, the person, the character you were meant to be. And, on another note, we're just in between plays. The slate is clean.

MARY ANN. Between plays. You mean another Beebles play?

BRANNON. Oh, yeah. Much more . . . *intense* than "The Accord."

MARY ANN. And we're in . . .

BRANNON. Transition between the first two main shows.

MARY ANN. The *first* two . . .

BRANNON. *Main* shows.

MARY ANN. So this is . . .

BRANNON. A show. Right.

MARY ANN. Just not a . . .

BRANNON. *Main* one.

MARY ANN. (*Confused*) Brannon . . .

BRANNON. I know. It's confusing.

MARY ANN. Yeah.

BRANNON. If you think fiction is confusing, you ought to visit the world out there (*motioning to the audience*) the world of reality as people out there live it. There are no openings and closings, no intermittent musical numbers, no special lighting, no retakes or rehearsals, just life and death, and it just keeps on going.

MARY ANN. I don't see how they do it. This alone is enough to . . . alone.

BRANNON. What?

MARY ANN. Where is everyone else? Wait. Where's Beebles? She was just over there.

BRANNON. Colton has already taken her. You probably heard, but he's met someone.

MARY ANN. Someone? Someone worthy of him, a nice, good-looking . . .?

BRANNON. A beautiful young woman.

MARY ANN. What?

BRANNON. Yep. Shocked us all. But hey, doesn't matter to me. To each his own.

MARY ANN. He's a good guy. Talented. And so are Michael and Piddles and Hatch and Match. And, oh yeah, Montaño. So good.

BRANNON. Montaño just contacted the local minor league baseball offices. He wants to take his shot at ball.

MARY ANN. Baseball? But he's . . .

BRANNON. A character. I know. There has to be a reason.

MARY ANN. But he's not currently in a play about baseball. If he's a character, how can he just go in another direction outside the stage. He can't.

BRANNON. Unless it's all a part of his characterization. You know, preparation for things coming. Background.

MARY ANN. You and your playwright.

BRANNON. He's your playwright, too.

MARY ANN. Montaño's got a lot to offer. Piddles is so dedicated. Michael's coming into his own. Agatha has her mysteries to solve. Colton has Beebles. Match and Hatch have each other. You're just Brannon. Just look at you. And Law is so certain of reality. And then there's me.

BRANNON. Mary Ann.

MARY ANN. Certain of nothing. I don't even know why I was written.

BRANNON. Everybody loves you.

MARY ANN. "Tolerates" is more like it.

BRANNON. Not true.

LAW. (*Entering from stage left*) This is what psychology books call an existential crisis.

MARY ANN. Oh, Law. I'm glad you're here.

LAW. Hello to you, too, Mary Ann. Cheers, Brannon.

BRANNON. Bonjour, Monsieur Avocat.

MARY ANN. This is more than an existential crisis. I was not placed well.

17

LAW. Questioning your existence and the reasons behind it?

MARY ANN. This is *not* an existential outcry. You should know better than that. Not everything is black and white, not even the law.

LAW. Daggers to the heart, my fair lady.

MARY ANN. Seriously. You know law exists only and absolutely to provide justice.

LAW. Wait a minute. It's there . . . it is established to provide for . . . oh.

BRANNON. You're wise, grasshopper. See. You have purpose in excess.

MARY ANN. I'm there for the dizzy laughs, "to swell a progress, start a scene or two, advise the prince no doubt, an easy tool, deferential, glad to be of use, politic, cautious, and meticulous; full of high sentence, but a bit obtuse; at times, indeed, almost ridiculous—almost, at times, the fool."

BRANNON. T. S. Eliot.

LAW. *Prufrock*

BRANNON. No *fool* can do *that*, Mary Ann.

MARY ANN. *(Beat.)* I want out.

LAW. What?

MARY ANN. I want *out*.

BRANNON. Mary Ann . . .

MARY ANN. I'm not asking to disappear, to be erased, or even to die.

BRANNON. Well, around here, death is no guarantee of getting out.

MARY ANN. Exactly. I want to be *written* out.

LAW. Written out?

MARY ANN. I don't want to be forgotten. I was in "The Accord." I was happy to be "of use." But as I am, I'm not who I should be. Maybe another form, maybe a play down the line: I don't know. I just want to be taken out, at least for a while. Gone. No more of this.

BRANNON. Are you sure that's what you're wanting?

MARY ANN. You know the playwright personally, right?

BRANNON. Well, yes.

MARY ANN. And he's writing this.

LAW. You're messing with my mind now.

MARY ANN. You're a character, too, Law.

BRANNON. Are you sure about this?

MARY ANN. It's being written *now*. True?

LAW. Wow.

BRANNON. (*Thinking*) True.

LAW. But if it's done, . . .

BRANNON. It's done.

MARY ANN. Good. All this, Colton's romance, Montaño's baseball interests, Michael's expanding leadership, even set ideas, they're all what? Not in the first play, not happening here—it's all backstory for the playwright, for his use in the next show, to fulfill his purposes, his theme, his goals. Well, here I am, being written out—by him. Now.

BRANNON. And so you are.

LAW. Wait. Is this legal? Is it just?

BRANNON. It's truth.

MARY ANN. So it is.

BRANNON. (*Breath.*) And so it's done.

Lightning flashes.

MARY ANN. And it's fair.

BRANNON. We need a short blackout, please.

The lights go out. The sound of the ocean increases. After a few seconds, the lights come back on. Mary Ann is gone.

LAW.   What just happened?

BRANNON. I love the beach.

LAW.   The beach?

BRANNON. Yes. I was thinking early about the sound of the waves and crispness of the air.

LAW. Do you know what just happened here?

BRANNON. On this beach?

LAW. No, on this stage. (*Then quickly*) And please don't stomp.

BRANNON. Mary Ann got what she wanted, and the playwright did what he needed to do.

LAW. But the consequences *of* that action, the repercussions *from* that action, what does it mean for any of us?

BRANNON. Law, you're written to be who you are.

LAW. I get that. I get most of this. It's logical. It's just a lot to digest.

BRANNON. We're characters. We've always been characters. Actors play us for the sake of our existence. And we live. Here.

LAW. For this moment.

BRANNON. For as many times as it comes.

LAW. And for justice.

BRANNON. We get to live. We actually have free will to develop as unique personalities.

LAW. So, this is a beach now?

BRANNON. I'm thinking so. The waves, the wind, the gulls.

LAW. A reference?

BRANNON. Probably.

LAW. You don't know?

BRANNON. Not this time.

Three characters, dressed in beach bathing suits, enter the stage. One is carrying a palm tree. One brings a treasure chest. The tree and chest is placed DL.

LAW. We may be about to find out.

One of the characters brings BRANNON a pirate shirt, a black mask, and a bandana.

BRANNON. Ah! Look at this. It's exhilarating not knowing what to expect. But, this narrows it down a bit.

BRANNON steadily and deliberately puts on the garb.

The character also attempts to give LAW a pirate hat and a sash.

LAW. (*Refusing the garb*) Uh. Um . . . no, thank you. Seriously. That's not my style. I'm sorry.

The character with the garb nods and then joins the other two nameless characters. They all exit.

BRANDON. (*Finishing getting changed*) Look at that free will in action.

LAW. Who were they?

BRANDON. Characters.

LAW. But who?

BRANNON. Minor, minor ones. Walk ons. Notice: no words. Just tasks. And swim suits.

LAW. A palm tree. A treasure chest. (*Walks toward the chest*)

BRANNON. Careful. We don't know the show yet.

LAW. *Treasure Island*?

BRANNON. Maybe *Penzance*. Perhaps we're the very model of a modern major character.

LAW. I do like that show. Extremely logical. Very precise in its interpretation of contractual law. Leap years and all.

There is the sound of a tinkling of a bell.

BRANNON. Is that what I think it is?

The sound of a clicking clock begins and then ends.

LAW. Then there's the clock.

BRANNON. You know what that means.

CAPTAIN. (*From offstage*) Pan! PAAAAN! (*Then entering. It is obviously Captain Hook from the Peter Pan tales*) Tick-tock, tick-tock, keep it away. Keep it away. (*Noticing BRANNON and LAW*) Aye. And who are you two? I don't recognize you.

BRANNON. We're new to the . . . area, looking for a band to join.

CAPTAIN. A band to join.

LAW. The backstreet is full, and we're just not in sync enough to join many others. We're just new kids on the block, 98 degrees from one direction, boys, no, 2 men in a savage garden, looking for a place to call our own.

CAPTAIN.   (*Confused*) What?

BRANNON.   Stop. *(Beat.)* Never do that again.

CAPTAIN.   Is something wrong with him?

BRANNON.   Not until now. It must be something he ate. Or thought. Or is.

CAPTAIN.   (*to Brannon)* Have you served on a crew before?

BRANNON.   Yes. I mean "Aye." And I'm happy to serve with you and Mr. Smee.

CAPTAIN.   How do you know my crew? And you know me?

LAW. Uh oh.

BRANNON.   Mighty Hook. Your reputation proceeds you. People all over tell the tales of
            your bravery to their children, of you and your noble crew.

CAPTAIN.   I don't know if that's true, but that's a good answer. (*He playfully hits Brannon
            on the arm, a bit too hard.)*

LAW. It IS true. Tales. To Children. Everywhere. Tales.

CAPTAIN.   (*Suspicious of Law*) Why are you dressed like that? You're no pirate.

LAW. This is a . . . a get up, a combination of pants and jacket that . . .

CAPTAIN.   It's a suit. I know what a suit is. I've just never seen anything look that that
            before. Where are you from?

LAW. It's actually a new suit, brand new. Modern. In "The Accord," I wore something a bit
            different. I was dressed in . . .

CAPTAIN. "The Accord"? Is that a ship?

LAW. Not exactly. It's a . . . play, a telling of tales of our own, well, tales of great people, great
            characters from shows gone by.

BRANNON.   (*Walking up)* A ship of sorts. A . . . vessel we worked on and traveled quite a
            distance on. It had a talented crew.

CAPTAIN. I've never heard of it. Accord? Sounds artsy.

LAW. And time-sy.

CAPTAIN. I don't have time for this ridiculous conversation. I have a boy to kill. He wears
            green and flies about with a fairy.

LAW. If I had five dollars for every time I heard that.

BRANNON.   Law, please.

CAPTAIN. (*Angrily*) Law? LAW?! Are you an officer of the law?

LAW. Well, that's usually my line, exactly.

CAPTAIN. (*Drawing his sword*) I hate the law. It stands for everything I'm against.

BRANNON. Put the sword down, Hook.

CAPTAIN. That's CAPTAIN Hook to you, and you don't tell me what to do! I'd as soon cut your heart out as to look at you.

LAW. Now hold on! This is getting out of hand.

CAPTAIN. Did you say *hand*?!

BRANNON. Great.

LAW. Oh, I'm sorry. I meant to say that . . . we . . . we just need to calm down. No need to fly off the cuff. Oh, sorry. I mean . . .

CAPTAIN. I've had about enough of you.

BRANNON. Captain Hook, listen. We know you're looking for Peter. We haven't seen him, but we'll help you look for him.

CAPTAIN. No. No. You're in cahoots with 'im. You're helping the Lost Boys. You're from Neverland.

BRANNON. Not at all. We're never seen Pan or been to Neverland.

CAPTAIN. I can spot a liar a mile off. And the only think I hate more than the flying twit is someone who lies to my face.

LAW. Listen here.

CAPTAIN. No, I take that back. There's one thing I hate more, an officer of the law.

The CAPTAIN approaches LAW, who backs up toward the treasure chest.

BRANNON. Wait a minute, Hook.

CAPTAIN. (*Still approaching Law*) CAPTAIN Hook.

LAW. Wait a minute here.

CAPTAIN. I hate officers of the law and kill them on sight, just like a pan.

LAW, falls back onto the treasure chest.

CAPTAIN. My chest! My treasure chest!

LAW. *Your* treasure chest? It's been sitting here . . .

CAPTAIN. So, defying me, lying to me, and stealing from me, too. And an officer of the law.

LAW. Take it. Take it all. They just brought it out. It hasn't been here long.

CAPTAIN. Oh, I'm going to take it. But that's not all I'm going to take.

LAW. Stop it. This is enough.

BRANNON. Stop it.

CAPTAIN. (*To LAW*) I've had enough of you! (*He pulls back his sword to kill LAW, who braces himself for the kill.*)

As the CAPTAIN thrusts his sword, he throws his head back, and he starts laughing loudly and maniacally.

BRANNON screams "NO!" and jumps in, taking the deathly sword thrust meant for LAW.

As BRANNON falls to the floor, the CAPTAIN is still looking up and around laughing victoriously while LAW, realizing what has happened, screams "NO!", falls to his knees, and embraces the dying BRANNON.

The CAPTAIN, losing his mind, sees both characters on the floor, assuming they both received death wounds, laughs more and screams, "NO ONE DEFIES CAPTAIN HOOK!" He lifts the chest and runs off stage, laughing all the while.

LAW. Brannon. Brannon! Speak to me. Brannon.

BRANNON. (*Having trouble breathing*) Calm down. It's okay.

LAW. You're going to be all right. It'll be okay.

BRANNON. No, I've lived this chapter before. Twice before. This is a bit more . . . serious.

The characters in bathing suits enter to remove the tree and anything left over from the previous scene.

LAW. I don't know what to do. I feel helpless.

BRANNON. There's nothing to do. It is what it is.

LAW. (*Slowly, dazed*) What it is.

BRANNON. (*Getting weaker with each line*) You repeat well. That's why you're good at line memorization.

LAW. That's an actor's tool. I'm a character, remember?

BRANNON. Oh, yeah. Aren't we all?

LAW. You saved my life. He was going to . . . kill me.

BRANNON. You would have done the same for me.

LAW. I think so. (*Beat*) I hope so.

BRANNON. I know so.

LAW. He just ran off. He thinks he killed us both.

BRANNON. He's a bigger moron than I remember. I'll bet it's a fun role to play, though. (*Laughs*)

LAW. As an actor? Or as a character?

BRANNON. A character playing a character. That's what we do on this stage, right?

LAW. Right.

BRANNON. I'm about gone now. I don't sense a resurrection this time. I think this little play's about over.

LAW. I guess it . . . is. (*Looks around*) It is.

BRANNON. You know. You're not too bad for a lawyer. I know you, Monsieur Avocat. You have a heart for justice. Go get 'em, Counselor. (*Looks up*) What a bright light. (*Beat*) Oh, it's a Fresnel. (*He dies.*)

LAW.   Brannon. (*Calming*) Brannon.

Two male characters wearing white swim clothes come out and gently carry BRANNON's body offstage.

LAW watches respectfully and intently.

After they are gone, LAW looks around at the empty stage and then out over the audience.

LAW.   A character playing . . . a character. (*Pause.*) Playing.

As LAW listens, various sounds build: the music from a wedding march, the sounds of a baseball game, the words "Grover's Corners, New Hampshire," soft music with the line "Let Faustus live in hell a thousand years," the sound of knocking followed by "Knock, knock, knock," followed by the soft bellow of a cow.

LAW.   The sounds of progress. Fair enough. *(Beat.)* It's the play. *(Another beat.)* A chord of transition into the refrain.

LAW slowly exits stage right. Celtic music begins, and the stage goes black.

28

Lowery Christopher Collins (Chris) has been an educator and writer for over thirty years. He is currently a professor of English at Panola College in Carthage, Texas. He has taught at the high school, middle school, and elementary school levels and as an English and literature instructor at the college and university level. For several years, he was a high school theatre director and a gifted education consultant. He's been honored with several teaching awards, including the Young Audiences of Northeast Texas Outstanding Service to the Profession Award and the Kennedy Center's Steven Sondheim Award for being one of the most "Inspirational Teachers" in the U.S.

He is also an award-winning playwright of over thirty scripts, a weekly newspaper columnist, a short story writer, a poet, a pianist, a vocalist, a songwriter, a recording artist with Daywind Studios, the founder and artistic director of Stagelands Theatre Company, an aspiring novelist, and a (former) choir director. He's taught a variety of classes, from rhetoric and composition to literature to acting to the Bible.

He holds a Bachelor of Arts Degree in English and History and a Master of Arts Degree in English from Stephen F. Austin State University in Texas and has served on fine arts and gifted education committees as well as on a board of governors for a small playhouse.

In addition to his interests in teaching, directing, and writing, he has a fondness for lighthouses, windmills, filmmaking, salsa, sculpture, Flannery O'Connor, travel, dominos, guacamole, social media, genetics, Maine, landscaping, pillows, gospel music, Shakespeare, marbles, YouTube, quantum physics, movies, weird jokes, maps, trees, cold rooms, and Texas.

 He can be reached at mrchriscollins@hotmail.com,

on Facebook at www.facebook.com/tofferdreams,

on Twitter at "tofferdreams,"

and at his website:www.ChristopherCollinsOnline.com.

To view Christopher Collins's books and other writing, visit Ponderlake Publishing, at www.ponderlake.com.

30

www.ingramcontent.com/pod-product-compliance
Lightning Source LLC
Chambersburg PA
CBHW050922120626
46552CB00018B/3171